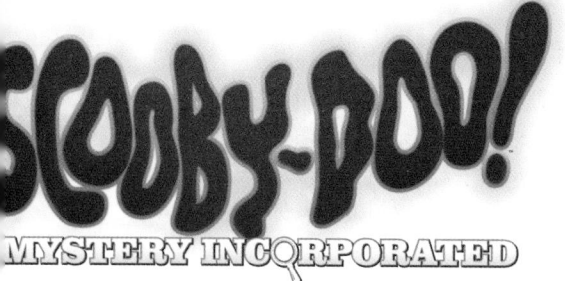

SCOOBY-DOO!
MYSTERY INCORPORATED

Beware the
BEAST FROM BELOW

250-750 WORDS

Adapted by Sonia Sander
Illustrated by Scott Neely

WORLDWIDE PUBLISHING

SCHOLASTIC INC.
New York Toronto London Auckland
Sydney Mexico City New Delhi Hong Kong

ISBN 978-0-545-31681-1

12 11 10 9 8 7 6 5 4 3 2 1   11 12 13 14 15/0

Printed in U.S.A.   40
First printing, July, 2011

The kids from Mystery, Inc. were on their way to school.

Just then . . . **BOOM!** A loud blast shook the road. A manhole cover flew up in the air. Fred slammed on the brakes.

R-O-O-O-O-A-A-A-A-R-R-R-R!

A slimy monster jumped out of the hole.
"Zoinks!" cried Shaggy. "What was that?"
"Let's find out!" said Fred. "Come on, gang!
Let's follow him!"

Fred led the gang down the hole into the sewers. A hole in the wall led them to a set of caves. Inside the caves, Velma found old barrels. They were dripping with green slime.

SPLAT!

Green slime dripped on Scooby, too.

"Ree-hee-hee," giggled Scooby. "Rop rit, Raggy, rat rickles."

But Shaggy wasn't the one getting slime all over Scooby.

It was three workmen trapped in cocoons!

The gang called the police.
The police really didn't want their help.
But the gang knew they could solve the mystery. So Fred stole one of the cocoons.
"Shaggy, start the van," called Fred. "I know someone who can help us."

10

The gang asked their science teacher for help.
Professor Raffalo examined the cocoon.
"He's alive, all right," said Professor Raffalo. "But
he seems to be frozen. I'll need to do more tests."

On their way home, the gang stopped for a snack. "Welcome to Fruitmeir's!" exclaimed Franklin Fruitmeir, the shop owner, "It's not ice cream, it's not yogurt, but it is delicious!"

"I don't get it, all this fuss over . . ." began Velma. "What is this stuff again?"

"Like, who cares?" said Shaggy. "It's delicious!"

The next morning, Fred went to see Professor Raffalo.
But Fred couldn't talk to his teacher.
Something strange had happened in the lab the night before.
Now the professor was stuck in a green cocoon, too!

The gang felt the case was at a dead end.

"We still have our first clue — the cocoon," said Velma. "I brought a sample with me. Hey wait, Scooby, what are you doing?"

"Like, it's Fruitmeir's!" said Shaggy, taking a bite. "The cocoon is made of the same stuff as the dessert!"

The gang had to look for clues at Fruitmeir's.
So Scooby and Shaggy went undercover. They got jobs at the shop. They let Fred, Daphne, and Velma in after hours.
The kids split up. It wasn't long before Scooby and Shaggy found the monster.

STORAG

17

RAAAAAAWWWWW!

"WHAAA!" cried Shaggy. "Like, run, Scoob!"

The monster chased Shaggy and Scooby all over the shop.

Meanwhile, Fred, Daphne, and Velma were looking for clues in the storage room. Until Scooby and Shaggy raced in, that is.

"Gangway!" called Shaggy.

"Roming roo!" called Scooby.

Shaggy and Scooby crashed right into Daphne.

Daphne fell through a hole in the floor. She landed inside the sewer caves!

"Jeepers," said Daphne. "Someone has been digging here."

Velma used her GPS to find out where they were.

"Jinkies!" she said. "This hole is under Crystal Cove Bank!"

The gang set up one of Fred's traps.

"We need to catch the monster before it steals any money from the bank," Fred said. "Is the trap all ready to go, guys?"

"Ready!" said Shaggy and Scooby.

Just then, the monster ran in.

SLAM! The cage landed with a thud. Only it didn't land on the monster. Instead it trapped Fred, Velma, Shaggy, and Scooby!

F-W-O-O-S-H! The monster blasted sticky goo all over them.

"Jinkies, we're stuck!" cried Velma. "Run, Daphne!"
Daphne climbed up toward Fruitmeir's shop. The
monster chased after her.

"Raphne!" cried Scooby. "Rotta rave Raphne!"
There was only one way out. The gang started eating.

R-A-A-A-H-H-H!

Up in the shop, the monster had cornered Daphne. But just in time, the rest of the gang escaped from the green goo.

SPLASH!

A blast of Fruitmeir's trapped the monster.

The gang was surprised when Scooby took off the monster's mask.

"Professor Raffalo?!" Fred exclaimed.

"That's right!" said Professor Raffalo. "I found the caves by chance. When I saw they led to the bank, I made my costume. Then I made it look like I was cocooned, too. It was a great plan . . . until you meddling kids and your dog came along!"

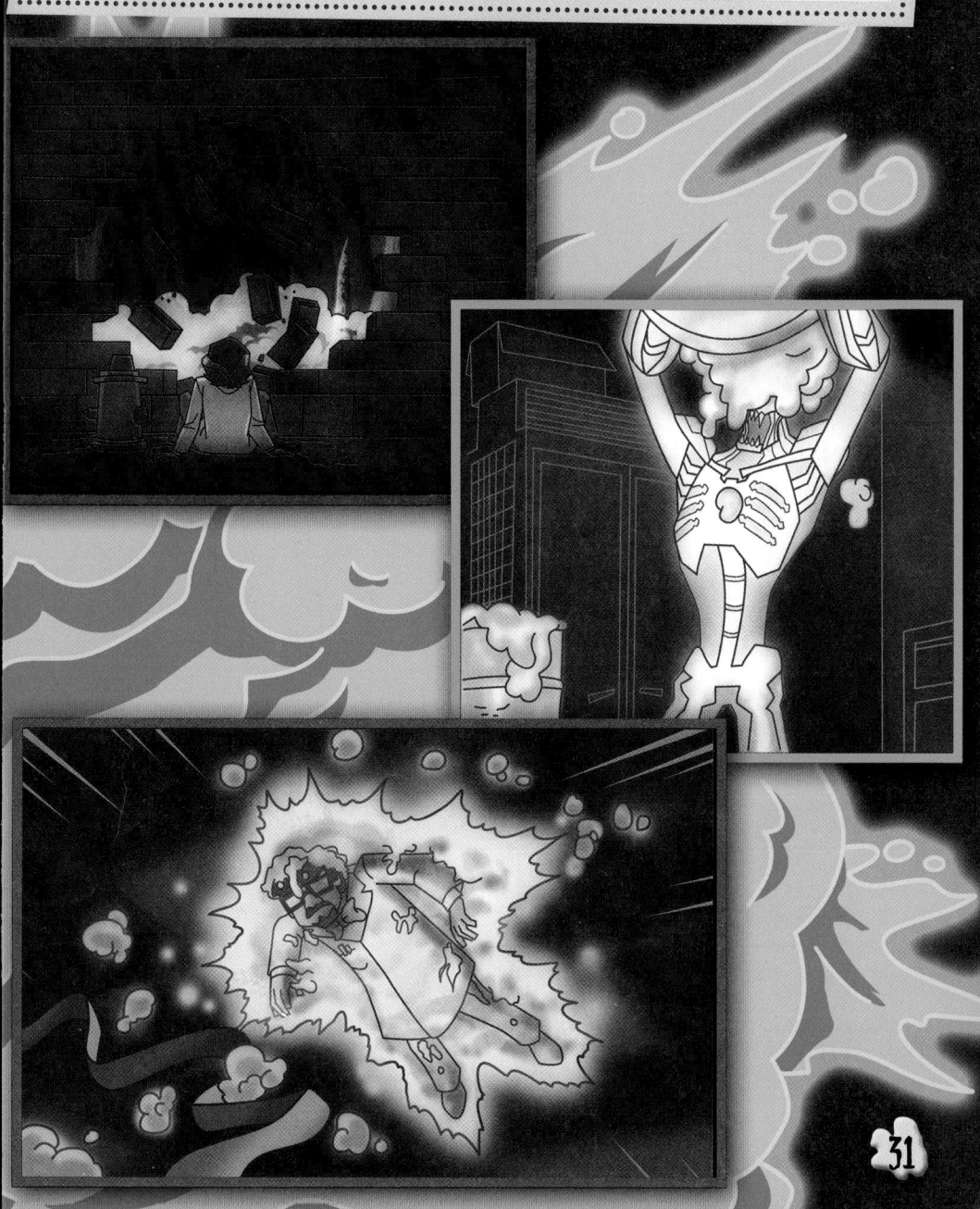

"You saved my store!" cried Franklin Fruitmeir. "Free Fruitmeir's for life!"

"Ranks! Rooby-rooby-roo!" cried Scooby.